HIT THE BALL DUCK

To Rikka

First published in hardback in Great Britain by HarperCollins Children's Books in 2005
First published in paperback in 2006

1 3 5 7 9 10 8 6 4 2

ISBN-13: 978-0-00-782720-6

HarperCollins Children's Books is a division of HarperCollins Publishers Ltd.

Text and illustrations copyright © Jez Alborough 2005

Visit our website at: www.harpercollinschildrensbooks.co.uk

Printed in Malaysia

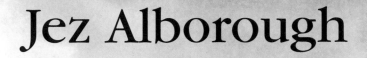

Jez Alborough

HIT THE BALL DUCK

HarperCollins *Children's Books*

Duck and friends are on their way, they're going to the park to play.

'We're here,' quacks Duck, 'I'll bat first. I'm so excited I could burst.'

Sheep, you catch it,

Goat says, 'Right, I'll throw the ball.
Frog can't catch, he's much too small.

Frog can shout, *'You've been caught so Duck – you're out.'*

Goat leans back, takes aim…and throws.
Duck shouts, 'WATCH HOW FAR THIS GOES!'

He swipes the bat –
they hear a SWOOSH!

Then with a C-R-A-C-K
the ball goes

WHOOSH! Up and up and up it flies.

'Catch it Sheep!'
the bowler cries.

'Where's it gone?' asks Sheep. 'Can you see?'
'Behind you,' cries Frog. 'It's stuck in that tree.'

'What shall we do?' asks Sheep with a frown.

'Climb up,' quacks Duck,
'and get the ball down.'

But the tree is too prickly, the tree is too thick.
Frog says, 'Let's knock the ball down with a stick.'

'Hold on,' bellows Duck. 'Use your head.'
'Why don't I throw the bat up instead?'

With a hop and a step
and a one, two, three...

Duck tosses the bat
towards the tree.

SWISH

goes the bat.

But where
does it fall?

On a branch, in the tree.
Now it's stuck like the ball.

'Too heavy,' says Duck. 'It went too low.
Let's look for something light to throw.'

That's when he spots the glove on the log.
'Oh no!' bleats Sheep. 'Stop him!' cries Frog.

But Duck bends down
with a one, two, three...

he hurls the glove
towards the tree.

WHIZZ goes the glove,
but where does it fall?

On a twig, in the tree,
with the bat and the ball!

Duck would like another go
but now there's nothing left to throw.

'Hey, I've got an idea,' says Frog.
'If Goat will sit here on this log,

then Sheep can climb up on Goat's back.'
'Don't forget me!' cries Duck with a quack.

With a hop,
and a step

and a one,
two, three…

Duck scrambles up
towards the tree.

'Now I can get them!'
he yells with a screech.

But the glove, bat and ball are just out of reach.
The game is over, or so it would seem...

then suddenly

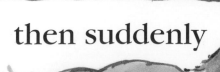

somebody else
joins the team.

'Hold still,' croaks Frog. 'I may be small
but I can make your team more tall.

I can do it, I can do it! I can reach all the way!'
That's when Duck begins to sway.

Down fall the team, Frog gives a jump,

then they land on the ground with a great big…

'Look,' cries Duck, 'we've wobbled the tree –
the bat and the ball and the glove have come free.

At last we can play, thank goodness for that. Come on –

it's still my turn to bat.'   'Not so fast!' they hear Frog shout…

'You've been caught so – DUCK YOU'RE OUT!'